Forced Adventure

by Chuck Nunes

Published by Chuck Nunes

This book is a work of fiction. Names, likenesses or other resemblances to companies, businesses, characters, places, and organizations are either products of the author's imagination or are used fictitiously. Any resemblance to any actual person, living or deceased, is purely coincidental.

Published by Banjango Enterprises,
Parris, CA
Printed in U.S.A.

ISBN: 978-0-09995612-6-3

To Joe Nunes

Chapter One

It was a crisp fall evening and Paul McCurdy was selling the evening edition of the Denver Post. People walking past on their way home would often buy a paper and passing cars would also stop just long enough to buy one. Paul would run up next to the car and hand the paper to the driver through the window.

World War II was going on, and there seemed to be American soldiers in khaki uniforms everywhere. Sometimes a soldier would ask Paul if he had an older sister or ask him to take a note to a girl he liked, and would often pay a nickel for the errand.

One time a soldier asked Paul to deliver a message to a girl standing on the corner, just across the street. Paul gave her the note and waited for her to read it. She asked him where he got the note, and Paul pointed to the soldier across the street.

"He's the soldier over there," said Paul, "the one leaning against the drug store building." To Paul's surprise, she walked back across the street with Paul and introduced herself to the soldier. They went into the corner drug store's soda fountain. Paul wondered what was in that note. It must have been the perfect thing to say, and he wished he knew what it was.

If Paul did not get all the papers sold on the corner, he would go to the saloons or bars in the area. They all had "No Minors Allowed" signs over the door, but Paul, who had just turned twelve, and was small for his age was never told to stay out, and he often wondered why they did not want people who worked in mines in there.

He would walk along the bar, yelling "Paper, paper, evening paper." Some of the men sitting at the bar would turn around and say things like "I'll take one kid," and give him a nickel. "Keep the change, son," some said. Or sometimes they gave him money for the paper and say, "Just keep the paper and sell it again."

Paul's brother Joe would usually show up and take a few of his papers to sell wherever he could. Joe was two years younger than Paul, almost as tall and was very thin. The brothers were very close as brothers often are, and they were also great buddies. Their friends all knew that if they hurt or bothered Joe, they would have to deal with his brother Paul. However, Joe was also a great tease, and Paul often had to intervene to keep his little brother from getting hurt by a much older boy.

Paul was the oldest child in a large family that had recently moved into an apartment complex they called "The Housing Project." It did not take the two boys long to find the community swimming pool where they learned to swim before the summer was over.

Their father had always wanted to be an artist and had studied and practiced painting most of his life. He was planning to go to France and join an artist community when he turned twenty-one, but that was before he met the beautiful girl who would become his wife. He decided right then and there to raise a family instead.

Paul was the first-born and brother Joe arrived eighteen months later. Siblings then seemed to be born about every year after that. Sign painting was about the only work Mr. McCurdy could find to support his growing family in the post-depression years. They sometimes went for days without much food, surviving on nothing but potato soup to "take away the hungries," as their Irish grandmother, who lived with them, often said.

Mr. McCurdy had been raised Catholic and insisted that his children attend the nearby Catholic school, St. Elizabeth, which admitted anyone regardless of income or ability to pay tuition. Paul had learned that the family was considered a charity case. For that reason, he wanted to go to public school, but he knew that his strict father would never allow that.

The services were often very elaborate, and the priest always prayed in Latin. Joe and Paul had good "boy soprano" voices and were very welcome in the church choir.

Paul loved school, but only so that he could play sports with his fellow students. He loved them all: football, basketball, whatever was in season. He also played ice hockey when the streets and nearby ponds were iced over enough for skating.

Someone had given him a pair of very large racing skates with extra-long blades. With two or three pairs of sox and a lot of paper stuffed into the toe, Paul learned to skate as good as or maybe a little better than the other kids.

In the classroom, he was considered a dunce. He was twelve years old and still could not read. Paul knew that he was missing out on a lot and would spend hours trying to figure out what the letters meant. The frustrated nuns would try everything—even the humiliation of standing in the corner—but he still never learned to read.

One nun who loved Paul and his artwork told him that he would eventually learn to read and that he had a condition known as dyslexia. "Just keep trying, don't you ever give up," she told him. "You are a bright boy. Don't let this one problem define you."

One day when Paul was selling newspapers on the corner his brother Joe came riding up on a bicycle! It was a shiny Road Master. Paul was very surprised. "Whose bike is that?" he asked.

"The people that live over in the next building gave it to me. They said that it was their son's bike, and he was a soldier that had been killed in Germany. They said that he would want the bicycle to be used by a good boy. I told them that I could ride to the store and do errands for them, and they just gave it to me to keep."

"That's great! Let me see how good it rides," said Paul, handing the newspapers to Joe. He rode a little way up the street and back.

"Man, it has balloon tires and rides easy. Maybe I can ride you on the handlebars, and we can go all over the place."

"No, I don't think so," said Joe. "It might get broken."

"Oh, it's a strong bike. Road Masters are the best, but they cost a lot of money. Don't worry, it will be okay. We see people riding double all the time."

"All right," said Joe. "Let's see how it works with two riders." Paul put his newspapers near the wall of the building and placed a big brick on them so they wouldn't blow away.

"Come on, Joe. Let's take a little spin, but keep your feet out of the spokes." Off they rode, two brothers now able to explore an even larger circle of their world.

Paul stopped selling papers when school was out, and the boys would leave home on the bike early in the morning and not come home until suppertime. Their mother was so busy with all the younger children that she did not even try to keep them home. Off they would go with Joe on the handlebars and Paul supplying the leg power.

Their world was now full of adventure. They rode the

bike to the museums, admired the paintings, saw the giant skeletons of dinosaurs, found the racetracks with horses in their stalls, and made friends with the black boys that cleaned stalls. They found the railroad tracks and talked with the hobos. They even rode out past the city limits, found reservoirs, and swam in farmers' ponds in their birthday suits. There wasn't a place within thirty miles of their home that the two boys did not visit that summer.

Chapter Two

When school started in the fall, Paul again sold the Evening Edition of the Denver Post on the street corner. One evening, a tall man in a long overcoat, his hat pulled down low over his eyes, approached Paul. He tried to hand the man a paper, but the man pushed it aside and flashed a shiny badge under his coat.

"I just got word over the radio that your brother was in an accident on his bike. He now is in the hospital with very serious injuries."

"No, that can't be my brother. He was just here," Paul protested.

"Well, what's his name?" asked the man.

"It's Joe McCurdy, but that can't be my brother."

"Yeah, that's what they said on the radio; Joe Mc-Curdy."

Maybe it is Joe, thought Paul; he rides that bike like

a wild man. I better get over to the hospital and see if he is there. Paul set the rest of his papers near the drug store building and put the brick on them. He intended to jog to the hospital that was just two blocks away. Then the man said, I'm' going to the hospital now. I'll give you a ride. My car is right over there."

Another man was in the driver's seat, and the tall man got into the back seat with Paul. "This is Poncho, my driver." After they had traveled a short distance, Paul noticed that they were going in the wrong direction. "The hospital is back the other way," said Paul, already a little concerned because the car smelled like a hospital.

"Turn around! Stop! Let me out!"

"Don't worry," said Poncho. "I know where we are going. Just relax."

They turned on to the main highway and headed towards the mountains, Paul was frantic, and he screamed: "Stop! Just stop and let me out!"

The tall man sitting next to Paul put his arm around him and held him tightly, putting a smelly cloth on his face. Paul quickly fell asleep.

It was very dark when he woke up. They were still driving, but now they were on a winding mountain road. The only lights Paul could see were those of the occasional oncoming cars. "Please, please let me go," he begged. "Where are you taking me?"

The men said nothing as Paul pleaded and then began to cry. When it started to get daylight, they were still driving on a winding road in the high mountains and pine forests. They turned off on a side road and drove back away from the highway and stopped. The men and Paul got out of the car and relieved themselves. The driver took a basket and a jug of water out of the trunk, and the men sat on the ground to eat.

Paul thought about making a run for it. He could hide in the forest and maybe find the highway. But it was a long way back, and he did not even know what way to go. After the men had finished eating, they told him to get back in the car.

"If you don't, we'll tie you up and throw you in," said Poncho. The tall man laughed.

Paul started running.

He ran into the forest faster than he had ever run before. They may be planning to kill me, he thought. I don't know why they took me. What is their plan? I can't let them catch me.

He was running for his life. He could hear the car coming closer and closer somewhere off in the forest. He took a sharp right turn and kept running until he thought his lungs would explode. He came to a steep hill and ran up. Run up this hill, he thought, maybe the car can't drive up here. There is no place to hide, not even a bush or boulders, just pine trees with tall bare trucks. Keep going uphill, But I can't! Got to hide, but where?

Paul came to a large clearing in the trees. On the other side of the clearing stood a metal structure with metal steps, attached to the side of a giant boulder. He heard the car coming closer and started up the metal steps. Up high, a deck circled a little house surrounded by glass windows.

From the deck, he could see an endless green forest far below, and he realized that this was a forest lookout post. There was no other way down except the stairs. He had trapped himself.

His captors watched Paul as he ran up the steps, and he knew that they had him.

The tall man called up to Paul. "We know you are up there. Come on down. We promise we won't hurt you."

"Come down here," said Poncho. "We can stay here all night, and it's getting cold. Make it easy on yourself."

Paul knew Poncho was right. He was already freezing in the cold wind, and it had started to snow.

"What do you want me for?" Paul yelled down to the men.

"Nothing. We just had a little wager. Poncho has won and the bet is over now. We will take you back to the highway and let you go," said the tall man.

Paul did not believe them. He crouched down and tried to decide what to do. He knew they would not leave. They were right: it was very cold, and they could stay warm in the car. He started down the stairs and then changed his mind. He went back up, hoping to get into the little lookout house, but the door was locked.

He sat down with his knees to his chin to warm up, but that didn't help. Snow blew sideways in a stinging wind. Paul knew that he could not survive there. He felt like jumping off the deck.

He finally decided it would be better to go back with the men. It'll be certain death if I jump and maybe they won't kill me. He decided to go back down and take his chances in the car where he'd at least be warm.

The men were quiet as Paul came down the steps. They allowed him to get into the back seat, again with the tall man next to him. No one talked as they drove back down to the highway where the sun was shining. Paul started to warm up.

After they drove back onto the highway, they came to a field of grass that seemed to have no end. There were no houses or buildings, just vast stretches of grass, separated by thin lines of willow trees.

As they traveled, Paul began to notice how beautiful the flat countryside and fields of grass were. For a moment, he forgot how much he missed his family. But then, he thought about his brother. What is Joe doing now? Will he get my papers from Mr. Peepers and sell them for me? A beautiful stream ran under a bridge they drove over, and Paul remembered trout fishing with his dad. It seemed like only yesterday. But now, these men had him, and it felt like he had always been held in this car with them.

Paul did not know why they took him or what they planned to do with him. But he decided he would never give up He would get away somehow. He would just have to wait for the right time.

Later they drove into a gas station, and Paul thought, now this is where I will get away. Poncho stayed with the car while the station attendant refueled it and checked everything. The tall man took Paul inside. When the man wasn't looking, Paul asked the store lady there if he could use the phone.

"There is a pay phone outside," she said. "Use that one."

"I don't have a nickel to get the operator."

"Well, I'm sorry about that, but this phone is not for public use."

The tall man, with his hat still pulled down low, came up behind him. "This is my son, and he is not very happy about leaving his mom. He will be okay when we get home."

Poncho came in and asked for a package of Lucky Strike cigarettes.

Paul could hear the Ford motor running just outside the door. His chance for escape! He ran out and got in the car and stretched for the pedals. He pushed in the clutch with his toes like he'd seen his father do, and pulled on the shift lever. It made a grinding noise, and the car didn't move. Finally, he got it into gear and moving slowly, but Poncho caught up with him before he reached the highway. He pulled Paul out of the car and punched him in the face.

"You little son of a bitch! I'm going to teach you a lesson. You don't steal my car." The tall man and the lady came out and stopped Poncho. Paul's eye and his nose were bleeding and the lady tried to stop it with a towel. "Just keep your head back."

The tall man repeated that Paul was his son. "He wants to stay with his mom in Denver. He will be okay when we get home," he said.

Paul yelled and screamed, "They are taking me away."

The tall man winked at the lady. "He's okay he is just a little spoiled."

He put his hands on Paul's shoulders and forced him into the back seat of the car with Paul holding the towel to his lip. As they drove back to the highway, Paul yelled, "Let me go? He is not my dad! Let me go!"

No one could hear him but his kidnappers.

Paul could see the sun sliding behind the snow-covered mountains in the distance. They would soon be in those far mountains. Eventually, they turned off the highway and followed a gravel road for mile after mile.

They finally came to a gate. An old Ford sat just inside the fence, and a man with long hair and a bandana on his head leaned against it. He looked like an Indian.

Poncho and the tall man shook hands with the Indian. The Indian looked at Paul. "He looks good," he said, nodding. "The missus will like him."

He took a wad of dollar bills out of his pocket and counted them into the hand of the tall man.

The two men then drove away. "Come on boy. You are staying with me now," said the Indian.

Chapter Three

Paul watched the car and the men go back down the road. He prayed that maybe now he would find a way to get back home. At least he could call his mom and tell her what had happened to him.

"You can call me Raven," said the Indian, as he closed the gate. "It's going to be my job to take care of you and make sure you don't run off."

Raven was a lean man, with long dark hair held back with a silver clip. He wore a bandana on his head and had high cheekbones.

"Come on, boy. Let's go meet the lady that owns you."

"What do you mean? Nobody can own me," said Paul angrily. "I have my own family and want to get back there right now!"

"Well, that's something you will need to take up with the missus. She just paid one thousand dollars for you, and she thinks you belong to her now. Of course, she is crazy, but I'm sure not going to tell her anything she doesn't want to hear. She packs a gun and has a very quick temper. Mrs. Stally lost her husband years before. When he died, she also lost her mind, and now she's very unpredictable.

"It is going to be my job to make sure you don't run off," said Raven. "I have also been told to teach you about ranching and how to take care of cattle because this ranch may be yours someday."

"I am not going to be here," said Paul. "I just want to get back home and be with my family."

"That can't happen now. There is too much hanging on you staying here."

"What do you mean?"

"Well," Raven said, patiently. "I'll explain it later. The crazy lady that owns this ranch happens to be my mother. But she thinks I'm only a half-breed accident."

Raven explained that his dad came from a nearby Indian reservation to work on the ranch, years ago, while the missus's husband, John Stally, was still alive. After John passed, the missus took Raven's dad into the main house to live with her.

She eventually had a baby but would not nurse or accept it as her son. The woman said that she would not have anything to do with a "half-breed" child.

Raven's dad named the baby and took him to the reservation where he was raised and went to school until he was twelve.

The boy grew up working with his dad on the ranch and learned how to raise cattle. When his dad passed, Raven was put in charge of the cattle, but the missus maintained tight control of everything. She sold off large parcels of the ranch and reduced the cowherd to about 150 head.

"Now," Raven said, "we only hire cowboys to help with the cattle for the spring and fall roundups."

Raven and Paul drove along the dusty dirt road until they could see some building off in the distance. A car was parked in the yard, and a tall, heavy-set lady in a long dress stood next to it, talking with the man in the driver's seat.

"That must be her legal man," said Raven. "She probably called him to come out from town and make you the next owner of the ranch. Lets just stay away until he leaves.

"By the way," said Raven continued, "those two men that brought you here also said that they would catch your little brother just like they got you if you ever try to run away."

While they waited for the legal man to leave, they drove up to an old stone house. Raven said it had been built many years ago by the first generation to settle the land.

"Now this is where you will live," he said. Inside there was an old bed, a rocking chair next to a fireplace, a table, and a stove. Cobwebs were everywhere, and it looked as if no one had lived there for a very long time.

"Let's go meet the old lady that owns you now," said Raven, chuckling at his little joke. Mrs. Stally was sitting on the porch and watched them walk over.

"Is this my store-bought boy?" she yelled. "He's so damned little! Are you sure he has been weaned off his momma's teat?"

Raven and the crazy lady laughed at that.

"What is your name, boy?" she asked.

"It's Paul McCurdy, ma'm, and I don't belong here. I was stolen and want to go home right now."

"Sorry, you are my property now," she said. "I paid good money for you, and you're not going any place. Raven better keep a handle on you, or I will shoot him dead, and he knows it."

"But, Ma'm, you can't just buy a person."

"Don't you tell me what I can and can't do, you little shit." She shook her finger at Paul. "This is my ranch, and it may even be yours someday if you can outlive me. I know Raven is thinking he will get this place when I'm gone, but now I have you in my will. Now, get out of my sight and go find something to do before I get mad."

"Come on Paul, let's go feed the horses," said Raven. They walked away. "The missus can be mean when she gets mad. The other day she shot and killed one of our dogs because the dog did not come to her when she called. That poor dog just had a litter of six puppies to feed. Her pups are still around here someplace, if the coyotes haven't eaten them yet."

They walked to another old stone building that Raven said was the icehouse. He said that it kept ice all summer because the walls were so thick and packed with saw-chips.

"We cut ice from the lake in the winter and put it in here to keep meat from spoiling." He told Paul that they had electricity for a refrigerator, but it was too unreliable, and a lot of meat had spoiled in it.

Raven cut a couple of thick steaks from a beef carcass hanging in the icehouse, and they went back to the old house. He cooked the steaks on the stove in a frying pan. After they had eaten, Paul lay down on the dusty old bed and fell asleep.

It was still dark the next morning when Raven woke him up.

"We're going to ride down to the pens," Raven said. "You just happened to arrive here in the middle of fall roundup. Let's go see how it's coming along. The cowboys should have most of cattle gathered by now."

On the way out the door, Raven asked, "Can you ride?"

"Do you mean to ride a horse?" asked Paul. "I have never even touched a horse."

"Well, you are going to ride today, because the corral is way off, and I'm sure you don't want to walk all that way."

They walked to an old barn with sun-bleached sides and a sagging roof. Two horses were inside eating. Raven led them out and tied them to a long rail.

Inside the barn was a little room for horse equipment Raven called a "tack" room. They each picked up a saddle and a pad, carried them out near the horses, and set them down on the ground. After the horses were brushed, Raven showed Paul how to put the saddles on the horses and fasten them down. He put a metal thing in each horse's mouth and said it was called a "bit" and was used to control the horse.

He handed Paul two leather strings that were attached to the bit and said, "These are called reins. We use them to tell the horse where to go. Now, take them in one hand and put your left foot in the stirrup and step up on the horse."

Paul looked confused.

"Here, I'll show you," said Raven. He stepped up into the stirrup, swung his leg smoothly over the saddle, and settled down on his horse.

"Now you do that," he said. It took Paul a couple of tries, but finally, he was sitting up high in the saddle.

They rode away from the barn and Raven showed Paul how to turn and stop the horse with the reins. He said that the horses were "well broke" and had been trained to do whatever a rider asks

They walked the horses down the road, passing a pond with cattails and lily pods. Finally, they came to a corral full of bawling cows. Ravel said that the hired cowboys had started gathering the cattle from the pastures before daylight. Paul also saw smaller herds of cows being driven down from the hills off in the distance.

Paul and Raven stopped at the pens. A big round tank in one of them collected water from a pipe in the ground. Raven told Paul it was a natural spring. They got down off the horses to drank water from the big pipe, but Paul could not walk right.

"My butt hurts!" he said.

"It won't hurt at all once you get used to riding." Raven laughed.

"When we have all of the cattle gathered, we're going to separate the calves from their mothers, and then they will be shipped off to the feedlot," Raven explained. "The mother cows will be given a shot and turned back out on pasture to make us more new calves.

"This is called a cow-calf operation. We only run about 150 head of momma cows now, but it still takes a lot of grass and fresh water to keep them healthy."

Raven got back on his horse and started riding away, and Paul rushed to get on his horse to keep up with him.

"That seems so cruel," said Paul. "Taking a calf away from its mother."

"Well, maybe it is in human terms, but that's just the reason we humans are able to live here on this earth. There are only two kinds of animals: wild and domestic."

Paul listened intently. The only animals he'd ever known were the dogs that lived in town with his friends' families.

"The wild animals all live and die according to the laws of nature," said Raven. "They can live high on the hog when there happens to be plenty of rain and food, but when the winter is severe, and when times are bad, many die off from starvation and dieses. That's just the way nature prevents overpopulation. Nature can be very nice sometimes, but she can also be very cruel."

Raven continued to talk as they rode up to meet the cowboys who were driving the cattle down from the hills.

"Many, many, years ago our ancestors started making domestic animals out of some of the wild ones to give them meat. Later they developed many different kinds of domestic animals to get all kinds of food, like milk and eggs. All domestic animals have a purpose. Even a little pet dog was made from a wild wolf because we wanted a pet.

"All of those cows out there are domestic animals, that we raise and take care of for our needs: and that is to give us food. Those calves were all born here and are yearlings now. They stopped nursing a long time ago and now are at least 400 pounds each."

Just then two big trucks drove up, each pulling huge stock trailers. They stopped near the loading chutes.

"They are here to haul the calves off to a feedlot," said Raven. "But they are early, we don't even have all the cattle gathered yet and we still need to separate the calves." He sounded irritated.

One of the drivers got out of his truck and went over

to talk with Raven. The other driver stayed near his truck, leaning on the fence, looking at the noisy cattle. Paul thought this might be my only chance to get a word out to his mom but decided not to tell the driver that he was kidnapped. He knew no one would believe him. He rode over to the man.

"That's a nice looking pony you have there, son," the man said cheerfully. "How is he bred?"

"I don't know what he is," said Paul. "But can I ask you for a favor?"

"Well, that depends on what the favor is. Do you want me to hold your horse, while you go take care of business?"

"No, but I do need to get a ride to the feedlot. I want to meet my dad there. Can I catch a ride with you?"

The man shook his head. "No. Sorry, but I'm not allowed to have riders. Something about insurance."

Paul was disappointed, but he nodded.

"I understand," he said. "Oh well. I will figure something out." Paul rode back to join Raven.

They watched the cowboys separate the calves from the mother cows and put them in a separate holding pen.

"Now we need to count the calves as they are loading on the trucks," Raven said.

The calves were put in a narrow chute so that only one could enter the trailer at a time. Raven gave Paul a clicker and said to push the little button for each calf as it goes on the truck. He had a clicker as well and said he would be doing the same thing so they could get a double count.

"Both clickers must have the same number when loading is complete," he explained.

When both of the trailers were loaded, the drivers started up their engines and moved slowly out to the road. The driver that Paul had spoken with gave him a big smile and a thumb up as he drove out to the road. Paul was disappointed and stood holding back his tears.

The next day, Raven and Paul saddled up the horses and rode back to the corral. Raven put the mother cows in a chute and vaccinated them before turning them out into a larger holding pen.

When he was finished, he got back on his horse. "Now we're going to drive the cow herd out to the range where there is plenty of good grass for them to eat," he said as he opened the gate.

"Come on, Paul," he said. "We need to ride around behind the cows and drive them out." Some of the cows were eating hay and did not want to leave. They had to be driven out of the pen.

Two cowboys also riding horses helped them drive the herd. It was late that afternoon when they came to a river, and the cows waded in to drink. The men got down off the horses and sat in the shade of a big pine tree for lunch. Raven opened a big sack of beef jerky and told everyone to help themselves. He told Paul it was seasoned beef that he had dried up to eat later.

After they had eaten and drank all the water they wanted, they gathered up the cows and started driving them ahead again. Soon they came to another big round tank full of water that was coming out of a big pipe in the ground like the one at the corral.

"That's another spring," Raven said. "We must have good water all over this range or the cow will keep grazing the same place and leave just weeds.

"Cattle and wild horses will only graze land within a few miles from their water source. Grass that is beyond that grazing distance won't get used. That's the reason we must have good water sources everywhere to make sure the cows always have good water. It's one of our most important jobs."

Chapter Four

The next day, Raven told Paul to saddle up. "We are going to ride the fence between the Radcliff ranch and the Stally ranch. Some of Radcliff's cattle have gotten over into our horse pasture, and the fence must be down someplace."

Raven and Paul rode along the barbed wire fence looking for a break. As they rode next to the fence, Raven would sometime get down off his horse and fix a sagging wire. Paul knew that Raven was his jailer but at the same time he was beginning like and trust him. He was learning a lot and liked the countryside.

"That land on the other side of the fence is Radcliff pasture," said Raven. "It's the biggest ranch in this part of the country. The missus has sold off a lot of her land to them. We still have some gates in the fence so we can move stock back and forth when needed. There is one of those gates up ahead, and the Radcliff headquarters is just a few miles west of that."

When they rode up to the gate, they stopped the horses, and Raven was very silent for a very long time. Finally, he said, "You know, Paul, trying to keep you a prisoner is a dumb idea. I just can't do it. I know the missus will be mad as a hornet, and I may get shot, but if you want to go, the Radcliff headquarters is just a few miles from here. Just follow the path to their place."

Paul was stunned. He couldn't believe what Raven was saying. Was he actually being set free?

Raven said, "Give me your horse's reins and walk along that trail to the house. I don't know what to tell the missus, but I'll figure something out if she doesn't shoot me first."

Paul got down off the horse and handed the reins to Raven. He watched as Raven turned and rode away leading Paul's horse.

Paul walked along the path. At first he was very happy, but then he started to worry. It was getting very dark and he couldn't see any buildings. The only light was from a million stars above. He could hear coyotes yipping and wolves howling off in the distance, and he wondered if Raven had been wrong. Was he lost in the middle of nowhere?

Then way off in the distance, he saw a tiny speck of light. He would be okay. As he walked, the dark outline of buildings became clearer, and light shone in the windows of one of them.

Two big dogs came running toward him, barking loudly. Paul did not know what to do and froze. The dogs sniffed him all over and started waging their tails. When Paul walked up on the front porch, the door opened, and a lady wearing a long white apron appeared in the light.

"Where did you come from and how did you get here?" asked the lady.

"Ma'm, my name is Paul McCurdy, and I was kidnapped. I just want to get back home to Denver."

"Oh, gracious me!" The lady covered her mouth with her hand. "Mr. Radcliff, come here, there is a young boy out here!"

Mr. Radcliff came to the door wearing jeans a leather vest and slippers. He had grey hair and was smoking a pipe.

"This is Paul McCurdy," said the lady. "He says that he was kidnapped!"

"Well, come on in and tell us about it," Mr. Radcliff said. "We don't get many kidnapped boys out here."

Paul followed them in past a big sculpture of a cowboy on a horse in the entryway and then into a warm lamp-lit room.

"Now, what's this about being kidnapped?" the man asked as he sat back in an easy chair.

"Well, I was selling newspapers on the corner in Denver when a man said that my brother was hurt riding his bike and was in the hospital," Paul explained. "The man said he had a car and told me that he would give me a ride over to the hospital. But then instead they headed up here into the mountains and I ended up at the Stally ranch. Mrs. Stally said that she had bought me and thinks I belonged to her. Raven was supposed to make sure I didn't get away, but instead, he just let me go."

"Damn, I always knew that old gal was off her rocker, but sure did not think she would do something like this," Mr. Radcliff said. "How long ago were you taken?"

"Well, I was selling papers Monday and I think it's Wednesday now."

"Your folks must be worried sick. We need to call them right now. They need to know you are okay. Don't worry son; I'm going to put you on a bus for Denver in the morning, but now let's call your folks. The phone is in the kitchen. Come on, I can make the call for you, what is your number?"

Paul gave him the number. Mr. Radcliff dialed and handed the phone to Paul.

"This is Mrs. McCurdy."

"Mom, this is Paul."

"Oh, Paul!" she screamed. "Where are you, are you okay?"

"I'm okay, Mom," Paul said, as he started crying with relief. "Some men took me up here to the mountains. I'm on a cattle ranch."

"Who took you?"

"A bad man told me that Joe was hurt and in the hospital, and he said that he could give me a ride to the hospital. But instead, he and another man took me up here. Is Joe okay?"

"Yes, Joe is fine. Have they hurt you? Where are you? We'll come and get you."

"I don't know where I am. Someplace up in the mountains. Mr. Radcliff, can tell you how to find this place." Paul handed the phone to Mr. Radcliff. Then he sat down on the floor with his back against the wall and his knees up to his chin as his mother and Mr. Radcliff talked. He covered his face with his hands and cried softly. Here I am twelve, he thought. Why am I crying? Everything thing is going to be okay now.

Mr. Radcliff hung up the phone and said that they had been disconnected. "I'll call her back later. Martha, show Paul where he will sleep. Carla and her mother won't be back tonight, put him in Carla's room."

Martha showed Paul a bedroom with colored pillows and a big comforter.

Martha turned the bedding back. "You can sleep here. The bathroom is on your right, next door. It has a tub in case you want to clean up, and I'll lay out some of Carla's nightclothes for you to wear. I think they will fit you okay. You can give me your dirty clothes, and I will wash them for you to wear in the morning. Just leave them in the hallway."

Paul did not know what to say. He was hungry, but he was also too tired to ask for anything to eat. He said,

"Thank you," and got into bed.

The next morning Paul found his clothes neatly folded in the hallway next to the door. He dressed and went down to the kitchen and joined Mr. Radcliff and Martha. After breakfast, Mr. Radcliff said, "Come on, son, we are going to town and catch a bus to Denver."

When the Greyhound bus arrived at the Denver station, Paul's mother and father were there to meet it with a lot of friends and relatives. Even a Denver Post reporter was there, taking notes. They all asked questions at once— so many that he could not answer them in the confusion. They wanted to know what happened and how he disappeared. Was he lost? They told Paul that everyone, even the police, were out looking for him. After he had hugged and kissed his parents, Paul looked around for his brother Joe. He saw him, straddling his bicycle out beyond the crowd.

Paul ran over and hugged his brother.

"Come on Joe, let's get out of here."

"How did you disappear so fast?" asked Joe. "I saw you one minute and came back a few minutes later, and you were gone. Who hit you in your eye?"

"Well, get on the bike and I'll tell you all about it. You just will not believe it."

The brothers rode off with Joe on the handlebars and Paul peddling.

About the Author

Chuck Nunes was born in Denver and left home at thirteen to work on the Platte Canyon Ranch near Littleton, CO. He served in the Air Force for four years before attending college. He received a degree in industrial design and worked as an engineer at Rockwell International Corp. for thirty years before retiring. He raised and trained cutting horses for several years, and today lives in the hills outside of Perris, CA.

www.ingramcontent.com/pod-product-compliance
Lightning Source LLC
Chambersburg PA
CBHW032011120726
47902CB00014B/2087